KARADI TALES

A Pair of Twins

Kavitha
Mandana

Nayantara
Surendranath

They both were born on the same day, just a few minutes apart. One was a healthy three-and-a-half kilo baby girl whom her mother named Sundari; and the other, a 500-kilo elephant calf that the mahouts called Lakshmi.

All this happened at the back of the palace, at the elephant stables. Sundari's father, Muniyappa, was the chief mahout. And Lakshmi's father, Drona, was the star of the stables – the majestic bull elephant who had led the Dussehra procession through Mysore city for the last ten years.

Ever since she could crawl, Sundari's father carried her off
to the elephant stables to play with Lakshmi. The little girl spent hours
frolicking at the feet of her large 'twin sister.' And over the years, as
the difference in their sizes increased, they changed the games they
played together. When they both turned five, Sundari was a skinny
18 kilos, while Lakshmi weighed three tons, at which point sliding
down Lakshmi's trunk was the game Sundari enjoyed most.

The game Lakshmi loved was when Sundari pretended she was a mahout. The young girl knew just which part of Lakshmi's back needed a scratch. And unlike Lakshmi's actual mahout, old Rajanna, when Sundari cleaned Lakshmi's face, she never hurt the young elephant's eyes.

Of course, this was their secret. Sundari's father would have been furious if he found out. For him, being a mahout was a man's job. And that was reserved for his son, Vikram. Muniyappa had decided long ago that Vikram would grow up and take his father's place as the Chief Mahout, while Sundari would join the palace dancers, just like her cousins and aunts.

Muniyappa had no idea that Vikram, at twelve, had his own plans for his future. No smelly elephant stables for him.

Vikram hoped to join the palace band as the lead drummer – mainly because the best uniform went with the big drum!

At the temple complex where the girls practised their dances, Sundari tried very hard to be a bad dancer. She deliberately made mistakes and ruined the neat formations that the dancers created. It was only at the stables that Sundari's talents bloomed. By the time she was thirteen, she was so good with the elephants that the mahouts accepted her as a sort of unofficial elephant 'nurse'.

And if Lakshmi fell ill, nobody but Sundari could handle her. Her doctoring skills worked miracles with other elephants too. She knew how to calm the troubled ones into taking their medicines. When she dressed a wound, you could be sure it would heal fast. Yet no one guessed how passionately this gentle friend of the elephants secretly dreamt of becoming an official palace mahout.

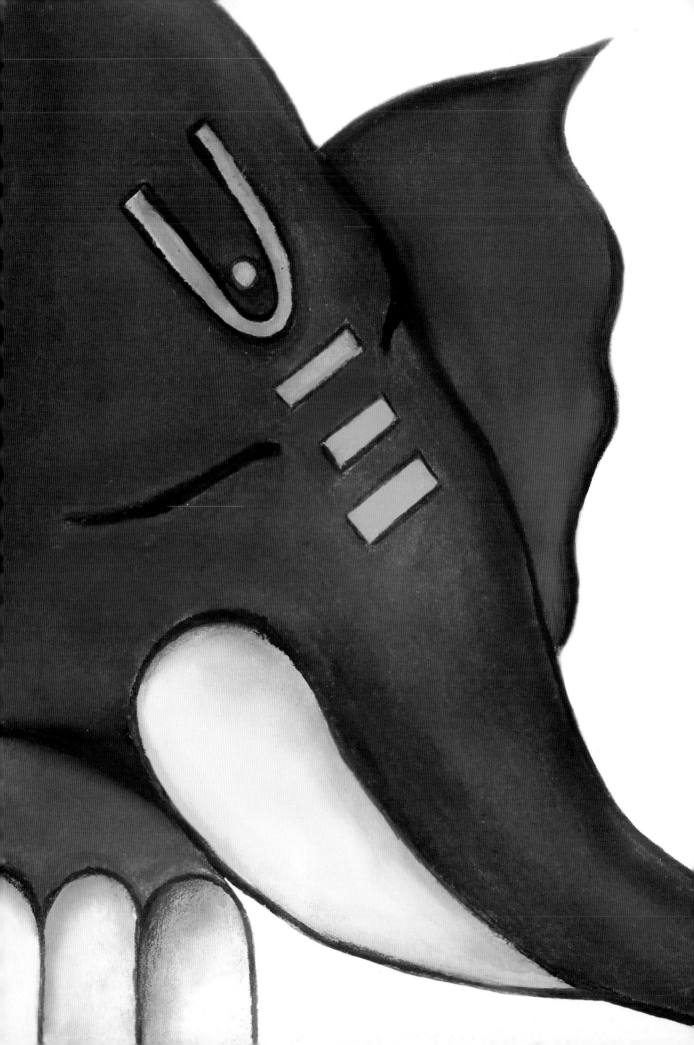

Normally, both the children's hopes would have remained empty dreams. But things began to go wrong at the stables. Drona, the hero of countless Dussehra processions, suddenly fell ill a few months before Dussehra. Now Drona was ancient, and elephants do fall sick now and then. But Muniyappa's problem was that none of the other bulls were as majestic as the old hero. Drona's own sons were disappointingly ordinary bulls, not at all the kind to lead a grand Dussehra procession.

Throughout September, Sundari nursed old Drona. If it hadn't been for her, the old bull might have died. But his recovery was slow and as October approached, the mahouts sadly realised that he would be too weak to carry the howdah.

It was Sundari who pointed out that Lakshmi would make a perfect replacement for Drona. But they all laughed at her, 'You couldn't have a female elephant lead the procession!' they guffawed rudely. Sundari shrugged her shoulders and chose not to reply. Lakshmi had, in fact, grown taller than her brothers and many young bulls. Sundari felt it was plain silly not to use her.

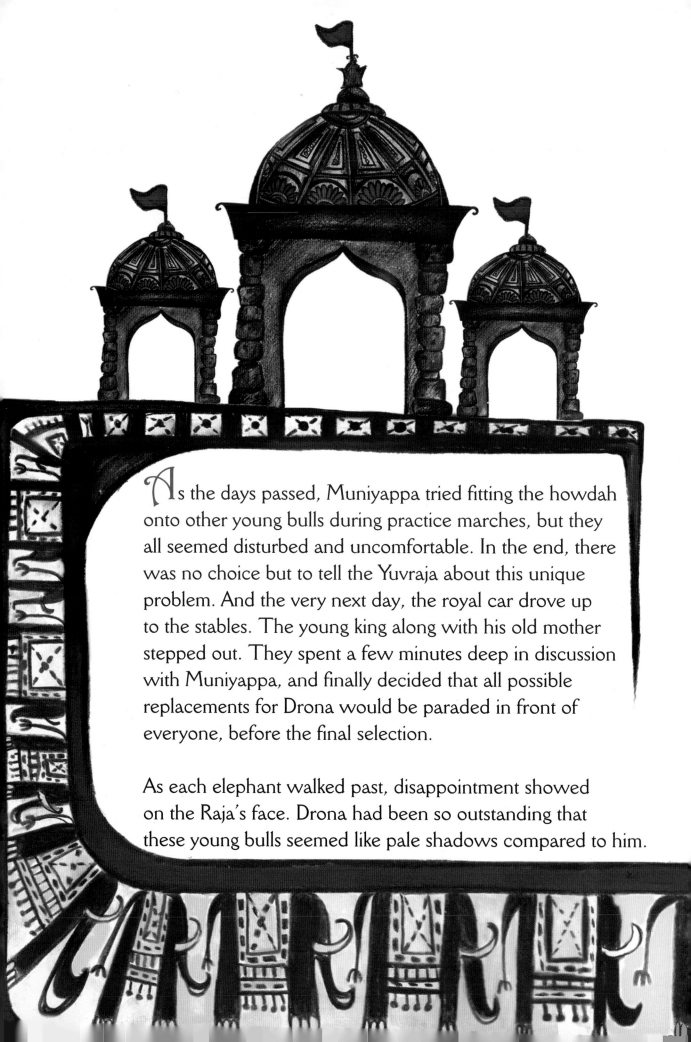

As the days passed, Muniyappa tried fitting the howdah onto other young bulls during practice marches, but they all seemed disturbed and uncomfortable. In the end, there was no choice but to tell the Yuvraja about this unique problem. And the very next day, the royal car drove up to the stables. The young king along with his old mother stepped out. They spent a few minutes deep in discussion with Muniyappa, and finally decided that all possible replacements for Drona would be paraded in front of everyone, before the final selection.

As each elephant walked past, disappointment showed on the Raja's face. Drona had been so outstanding that these young bulls seemed like pale shadows compared to him.

Finally, in spite of Muniyappa's protests, old Rajanna
paraded Lakshmi past the Raja. And his face lit up!
Here was Drona's heir, an elephant regal and graceful enough
to take over from him! Imagine the Yuvaraja's excitement
when he discovered that Lakshmi was, in fact, Drona's daughter.
It didn't bother him or his mother that for the first time in history
it would not be a bull leading the Dussehra procession.

With this important decision taken, everybody looked relieved.
Even those who had earlier laughed when poor Sundari
had suggested Lakshmi's name.

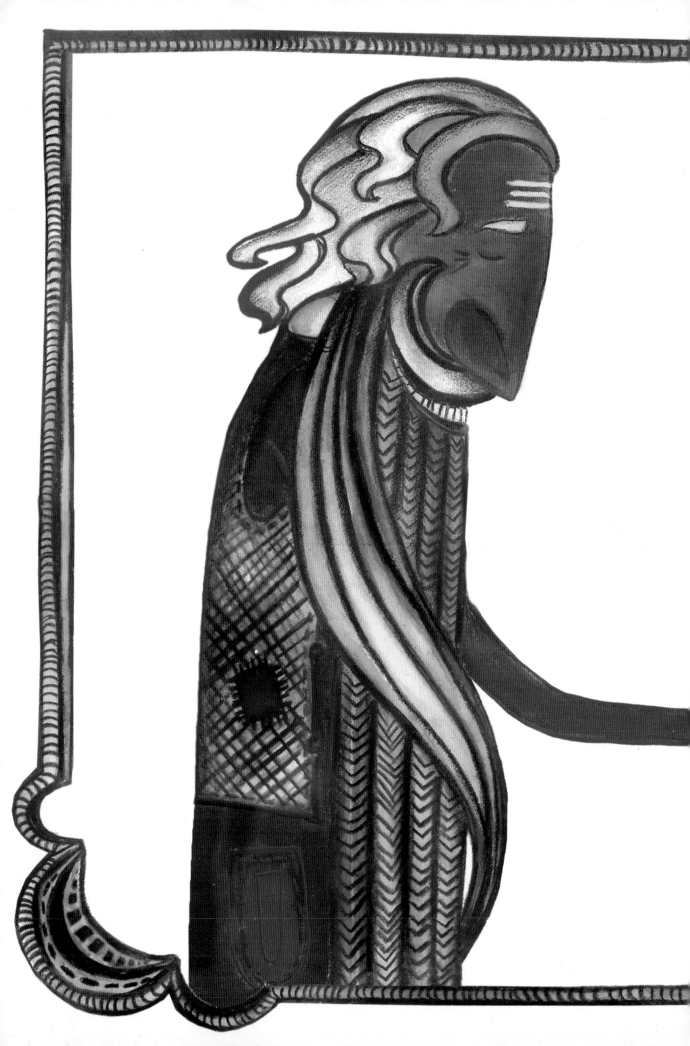

But soon old Rajanna began to fidget uncomfortably. He nervously asked the king's permission to make a suggestion. With a tremor in his voice, he told the Raja about how he was now a very old man. Everybody nodded in agreement. Rajanna was indeed very ancient. This kind of talk usually meant he was going to ask for some extra money or favour.

But he didn't. Instead he confessed that he was too old to wear the grand costumes reserved for the Dussehra festival, and would look pathetic seated on the elephant carrying the royal howdah. His other worry was that Lakshmi hadn't been trained to carry the howdah and walk at the head of a procession.

The king and his mother began to look worried all over again. Rajanna swiftly reassured them that thankfully there was one very able person who could train Lakshmi for her important task. When the queen asked who that was, Rajanna stunned everybody by mentioning Sundari's name!

All hell broke loose! Muniyappa himself stepped forward in a great temper and declared that it would be his son, Vikram, who would take Rajanna's place, and who was Rajanna to recommend anyone else. Vikram, meanwhile, broke out in a nervous sweat, yet somehow managed to tell the king that he couldn't control Lakshmi. In fact, he admitted to being scared of her! That got Muniyappa so furious that all the mahouts had to hold back their chief from beating up his 'silly band-boy of a son.'

Finally the Maharani's patient and soothing words got the tempers under control. After talking to all the mahouts, who each admitted that they couldn't train Lakshmi as well as her own 'twin,' Sundari was sent for.

When Sundari was brought before the royal family, the Maharani herself told the stunned girl about her new role. Sundari couldn't believe her ears. Nobody from the stables had ever seen this chatter box so tongue-tied!

She sneaked a look at her father to check if he was angry, but after listening to all the mahouts praise Sundari, Muniyappa couldn't help feeling proud of her. It was only natural that she had such a wonderful way with elephants, he decided. Wasn't she the daughter of Muniyappa, Chief Mahout of the Mysore palace? So what Sundari saw was not the furious father of a few minutes back but a proud man, bravely wiping away a tear from his cheek.

She turned to Lakshmi, who looked as if she had always known that the two of them were destined to lead the Dussehra procession through Mysore!

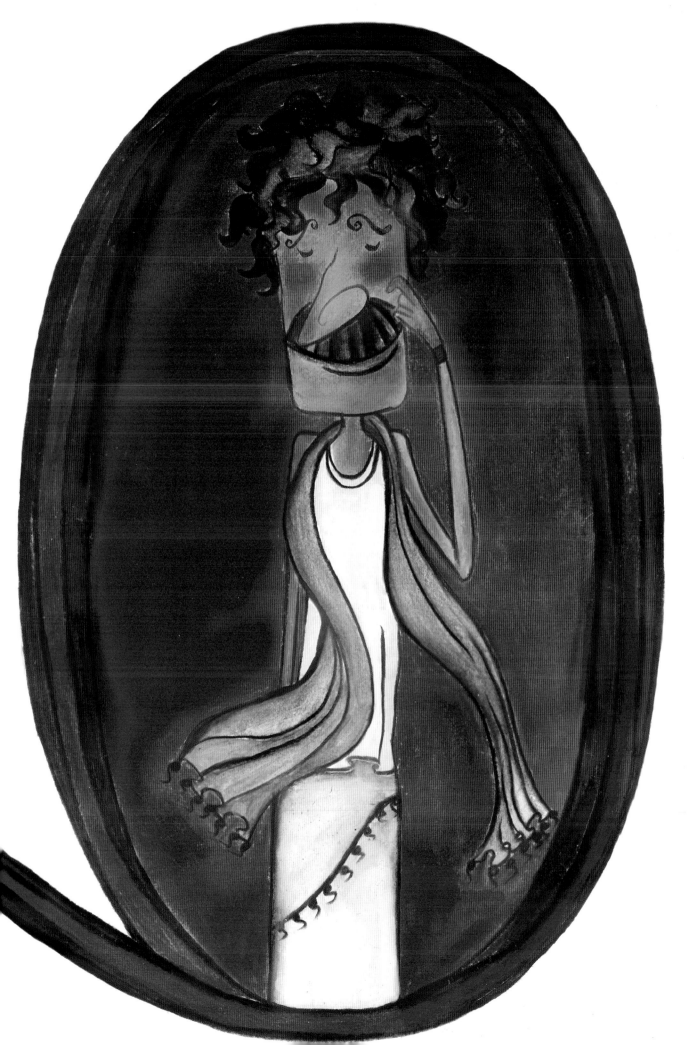

Finally, a grinning Sundari stepped forward to thank the Maharani. While the small crowd cheered for her, Muniyappa suggested that since there were no costumes for female mahouts, Sundari could just dress up like a man, hiding her plaits under a turban.

Poor Sundari was shattered, and her disappointment was so obvious that the Maharani immediately asked what had upset her so. Looking very determined, the young girl spoke up. She didn't want to dress up as a man, she said. If, for the first time in the history of Mysore city, a female elephant would carry the golden howdah, why couldn't a girl be the mahout, she querulously asked the queen, with tears almost spilling out of her eyes.

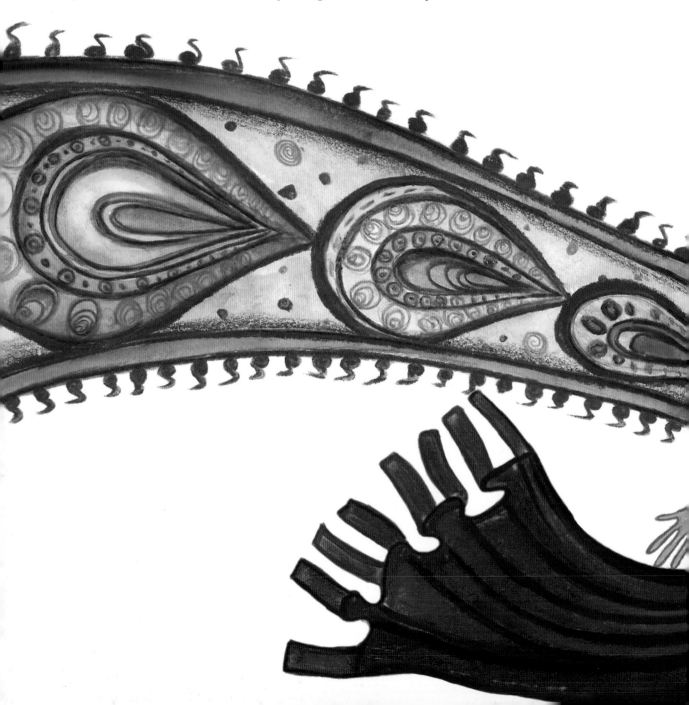

The old Maharani smiled at this young girl's courage to speak up. Why ever not, she asked herself. After all, the reigning deity of Mysore was not a God, but a Goddess – Chamundeshwari. Her fierce bravery had destroyed the demon Mahishasura, and pilgrims from all over India flocked to Mysore to get her blessings at her hilltop temple outside the city.

Yes, it would be just perfect for Chamundeshwari's idol to be carried through Mysore on a graceful cow elephant, ridden by a courageous mahout girl! Beckoning Sundari to come closer to her, the old queen whispered something into her ear. The young girl's face broke into a smile! But the queen's words were to remain a secret till the first day of the processions.

Over the following week, Sundari trained Lakshmi to lead the elephants with the heavy golden howdah on her back. And on the day of the procession, the fabulous traditional frontlet was attached to Lakshmi's forehead with great care. The jewellery was so heavy that tiny Sundari needed three muscular men to help her! Together, they draped yards of brocaded silk on Lakshmi's back. Finally, the famous golden howdah was strapped on. Then the priest performed a long pooja to Goddess Chamundeshwari, before placing the idol on Lakshmi's back.

Lakshmi was ready! Only then did Sundari dash off to get dressed. Nobody knew what this young girl was going to wear till she reappeared, excited and nervous at the same time.

She had flowers in her hair, and looked resplendent in her turquoise blue dancer's sari! That had been the queen's idea, she told everybody.

Though it looks like a sari, a Bharatnatyam dancer's outfit is actually cleverly stitched like a pair of pants with a set of false pleats that camouflage the legs – a perfect outfit for a young girl to sit astride an elephant!

On that first night of Dussehra, the crowds went wild as Lakshmi stepped out on to the main street of the city. Children had come from hundreds of miles away to see Drona's daughter walk tall – the first cow elephant ever to carry the Golden Howdah. And on her neck sat the city's young heroine – Sundari, the first girl to ever become a royal mahout and ride with Goddess Chamundeshwari.

Text: Kavitha Mandana
Illustrations: Nayantara Surendranath

Karadi Tales Company Pvt. Ltd.
3A Dev Regency 11 First Main Road Gandhinagar Adyar Chennai 600020
Ph: +91 44 4205 4243 Email: contact@karaditales.com
Website: www.karaditales.com

Distributed in North America by Consortium Book Sales & Distribution
The Keg House 34 Thirteenth Avenue NE Suite 101 Minneapolis MN 55413-1006 USA
Orders: (+1) 731-423-1550; orderentry@perseusbooks.com
Electronic ordering via PUBNET (SAN 631760X); Website: www.cbsd.com

Printed in India
ISBN 978-81-8190-302-0